The Best Spot In the Garden

Alexa Galan

Illustrated by Valeria Cervantes

MASCOT BOOKS

GreenTales

It was a beautiful day to take
a stroll in the garden!

The sun was shining, the birds were singing,
and the butterflies were twirling around
the Sarah P. Duke Gardens.

"Come on, sleepy heads," called Mommy.
"Wake up, so we can enjoy all the
beautiful things in the garden!"

DJ and Jenny enjoyed the garden
and knew they would have a lot of fun.

"Today we are going to play a game called
the best spot in the garden," said Mommy.
"How does that work?" asked DJ.

"Easy. You have to just tell me what
you think is the very best spot in the
garden," said Mommy.

"I know the best spot in the garden!"
said Jenny.

"It is right here in this big circle! I can run
round and round and see and smell lots
of pretty flowers!"

"I know the best spot in the garden!"
said DJ. "It is under this huge tree
with all those cool roots."

"I would like to be a squirrel and
climb all the way to the top!"

"I know the best spot in the garden!"
said Jenny. "It is this huge bird house."

"I can pretend I am a humming bird
and fly around the Duke Gardens."

"I know the best spot in the garden!"
said DJ. "It is right here in the fish pond."

"I can sit on these cool rocks and watch the different colored fish."

"But this must be the best spot in the garden!" said Jenny.

"Look at these stepping stones in this pond. You can jump, jump, and keep jumping from one to the other!"

Then, DJ and Jenny whispered into
each other's ears and they knew they
had the right answer.

They looked at Mommy and both said,
"We know the answer. The best spot in
the garden is next to you, Mommy!"

The End

www.mascotbooks.com

For more information, please contact:
Mascot Books
P.O. Box 220157
Chantilly, VA 20153-0157
info@mascotbooks.com

CPSIA Code: PRT1210A
ISBN-10: 1-936319-35-7

MASCOT BOOKS is a registered trademark of Mascot Books, Inc.

Printed in the United States

About the Author

Alexa Galan is currently a junior
at Duke University, and ultimately,
a kid at heart. Having always been
an avid reader and lifelong lover of
literature, Alexa made the transition
into storytelling by recently
publishing her first two children's
books. It was the captivating beauty
of the Sarah P. Duke Gardens that
inspired Alexa to write this book
and encourage young readers
to walk through and enjoy the
garden's special grounds.

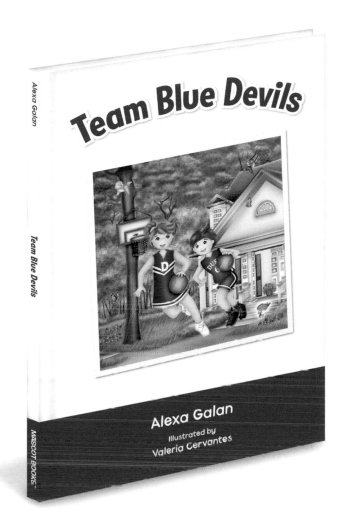

If you enjoyed this book, you might
also enjoy *Team Blue Devils*,
written by Alexa Galan.